I am a BIG GIRL now!

Ankita Sanghi

This is a work of Fiction. Names, characters, businesses, places, events and incidents are either products of the author's imagination or used in a fictitious manner. Any resemblance to actual persons, living or dead, or actual events is purely coincidental.

First Edition: June 2021

Typeset in Adobe Garamond Pro

ISBN: 978-93-91116-56-9

Cover Design: Prashant Gopal Gurav

Publisher: StoryMirror Infotech Pvt. Ltd.
145, First Floor, Powai Plaza, Hiranandani Gardens, Powai,
Mumbai - 400076, India

Web: https://storymirror.com
Facebook: https://facebook.com/storymirror
Twitter: https://twitter.com/story_mirror
Instagram: https://instagram.com/storymirror
Email: marketing@storymirror.com

To my dear readers and to all those

who made this book possible

Acknowledgments

I devoutly express my gratitude to the esteemed founder of StoryMirror, Bibhu Datta Rout, for providing this wonderful medium. I extend my deep appreciation to my credible editor, Divya Mirchandani for the mighty efforts that she had put in for this book, and to the entire team of StoryMirror Publications for their unwavering support and guidance.

Special thanks to the calm and composed Meet Jain for giving instant solutions to all my queries in this whole publishing process.

My parents, my family, my friends, I am truly grateful to each and every one who encouraged me and has been with me all through in my journey of writing.

Author's Note

Being an ardent observer, I get influenced by every little thing around me. A difference in the human nature, behaviour, character, culture, and such many more traits fascinate me. When I listen to people's stories, I understand that every happening has some deep meaning lying within it. Every experience, whether it's happy or sad, has a learning behind it. This book is a result of such heart-warming realizations.

These fables are inspired from incidents that had either occurred with me or with my loved ones. Although the names of the characters have been changed for the protection of their privacy, the emotions weaved in the stories are absolutely genuine. Some of these stories present innocent adolescence, some of them portray people who had courageously fought with the adversities of their life, while some represent those who had fallen prey to a vice. Some represent people who learned a lesson from their mishappenings, and then there are those people who set an example for others. Some stories gently throw a light on social issues prevalent around us. All in all, there are many moments that will strike a chord with you, and I hope you will be able to identify yourself in the fables. And when it does, do spare some time to drop me a mail. Would love to hear from you.

Happy Reading!

Contents

I am a Big Girl now!

Diya, a young woman of 22 years was fondly enjoying the cool fragrance and soft music at *Aangan resorts*, Jaipur. With beaming coloured bulbs and floral decor, the resort looked magnificent. It was the summer break and Diya was here to attend her cousin's wedding. This wasn't the first time she was here and this place did bring back some daunting memories. She was seated in front of the stage which had two huge chairs with red upholstery and silver embellishments that made them look like a throne, arranged for the couple to be wed. She was gazing at them intently when all at once, her mind drifted to the incident which occurred when she was here for the first time ten years ago.

Diya lived in Hyderabad with her parents, Raman and Pooja Mittal. Raman was a very amicable person whereas Pooja was a rational lady with strong convictions. Diya was 12 years old when her dearest cousin's marriage was fixed. She jumped for joy as she heard the news. But there was a small hitch. The wedding was decided to be held in Jaipur. Her mother would not be able to make up for the wedding as she had a hysterectomy surgery about a week ago and was not allowed to travel. Mr. Mittal decided to go along with their relatives who would travel by train. When Diya got to know that her mom could not accompany her, she was disheartened. The doting father could not see her daughter sad, and thus persuaded Diya to attend the wedding with him. Pooja was not convinced with this idea and was worried for her daughter. She explained to her, "Beta, try to understand, you have never been without me anywhere. Papa will be busy over there. It will be difficult for you dear". But Diya was in no mood to listen. She said emphatically, "Don't worry Mumma, *I am a Big Girl now!*" Looking at her innocence and strong wish to attend the wedding, Pooja smiled and gave her consent. She double checked her daughter's suitcase and made sure that all the necessities were packed properly. Diya was totally exhilarated, not just for the wedding, but for the train journey as well, as she would get to read her favourite comics and a variety of refreshments at different stations.

It was time to leave for the railway station. Diya, who was very happy and enthusiastic till now, suddenly became too emotional. She cried like a young bride leaving her home. Tears rolled down through Mommy's cheeks too. She hugged her loving daughter, wiped her tears and said, "you said you are a big girl, and big girls don't cry right!". Diya cheered up and left with her father. Soon they boarded the train to Jaipur. She was elated to find that she would travel along with their extended family members and friends.

Among the family friends was Nitesh, a tall, well sculpted young man in his 20's whose berth was next to Raman. He warmly greeted everyone and then looked at Diya, seated opposite him. He had seen her last about two years ago when she was a kid. But now she was a naïve plump girl blossoming into a woman. He checked on her from top to bottom. Her angelic eyes with a beaming smile perfectly synchronized with her bubbly outlook. She had a dark brown hair that flawlessly matched her light-toned skin. Nitesh was awestruck and stared at her savagely. Diya sensed this and was quite uncomfortable, however, she politely greeted him, "Hello Bhaiya, how have you been?" He greeted her back ignoring the word 'bhaiya'. The long train journey and Nitesh's pleasant and amiable behaviour, rendered him close to this father and daughter duo. Early the next evening, they reached their destination, Jaipur. A wedding bus had been arranged for their pick up and drop to the *Aangan resorts*. Diya occupied a window seat near her father. She was looking out dreamily, wondering about weddings and all the grandeur while Nitesh offered her candy and chips.

Wedding nuptials began the next morning. All the elders were busy in the preparations while kids were running around gleefully. Diya was wandering around the resort looking for her cousin, Swati. Nitesh caught her sight and he immediately walked up to Diya and rattled, "Hey dear, what are you doing here? Come, let me show you this beautiful resort". She was startled for a moment but then she denied him affably saying, "Thanks bhaiya, but I have a Sangeet rehearsal now and so I was just looking for my partner Swati". After dwelling on it for a minute, he lied, "Oh, I just saw Swati going this way, come, I will take you there". Diya silently followed him completely unaware of his hideous intentions.

He took her to a far corner of the resort. She began to panic, pleading for him to take her back to her dad. But nothing could stop him and he was burning with dirty passion. Before she could understand anything, he grabbed her tightly with his arms and tried to reach for her lips. Diya violently shook her head, not allowing him to kiss her. He then stroked his hand under her skirt and touched inappropriately while the girl saw the shamelessness and horror in his eyes. Diya fiercely fought, squirmed out of his arms and ran as fast as she could. Within minutes she reached her room and locked it from inside. She was still in shock and couldn't believe what had just happened.

For a child her age this was traumatic and left her anxious and embarrassed at herself for trusting a stranger. She closed her eyes in anguish and cried her heart out. Her first thought was to tell her father about it but then a concoction of fright and guilt took over her mind and left her paralyzed. She couldn't bring herself to discuss this with her father and thus she decided to keep it to herself. However, she was alert and made sure to maintain distance from Nitesh for the remainder of the trip.

Once the wedding concluded, the father-daughter duo was back home. Diya was extremely delighted to see her mom, who was waiting for them eagerly. Mommy hugged Diya affectionately and gifted her, her favourite Barbie doll which she had been longing for. Later that night, Pooja sat with her daughter, who she missed so dearly and asked gently, caressing her hair, "How was the wedding honey?" Diya gleefully gave a detailed description of the wedding shenanigans, avoiding Nitesh and the episode entirely. Raman had informed his wife that he sensed some awkwardness between Nitesh and Diya. So Pooja then trickily continued, "Papa told me Nitesh bhaiya also travelled with you and he was very kind and showered you with candies, is that true?" Diya was perplexed on the mention of his name and avoiding eye contact she hesitantly answered, "Umm.. er.. yes Mumma, he was nice".

Pooja immediately sensed that something was not right. She drew her loving daughter close to her, held her hands and said, "Don't be scared. Trust me and tell me everything". Diya instantly broke into tears but then summoned all her strength and opened up all about that disturbing evening. Pooja found this extremely difficult to listen to and was furious with anger. However, she did not express her rage in front of her daughter and at the end, she calmly said, "Don't worry dear, everything will be fine. Let's go to sleep now".

Next day, when Diya returned from school, she was terrified to find Nitesh sitting in front of her parents in her living room. Pooja held Diya and made her sit beside her. Her dad yelled angrily at Nitesh, "will you tell me everything by yourself or want me to call the cops?" The young boy was trembling with his heart pounding loud. He wiped the sweat from his forehead and confessed everything. Raman landed a slap across his face. And then once again, there was one more loud slap on the opposite cheek. The boy was in tears by now, pleading for forgiveness. Diya was happy to see her parents stand up for her and silently by watching this, she let out all her anguish and pain. She realized, she is a really a big girl now and had to be careful before trusting anyone.

Nitesh apologized to Diya and to her parents. Considering his sincere apology and the family's relationship with his father, Diya's parents decided to let him go with a warning to never repeat any such actions with any girl in future. Nitesh was guilty and he never met Diya again. Pooja's heart to heart conversation with her daughter gave Diya the strength to speak up and fight her fears. Their wise decision showed the boy a right path to walk forever.

Dear readers, we all come across such men every day and it is our duty as a society to help and protect our children and help them muster the courage to fight their fears. I want to emphasize the fact that it is equally important to educate our boys to respect women and educate our girls to stand up and fight back when needed. It's time to teach our kids to differentiate between good touch and bad touch. Although it may be difficult, please start the conversation about safety and private space with your kids when they are young and continue to engage teens in such conversations. Let us all pledge to teach our kids responsibility and help build a better world.

Upside Down

Social media has undoubtedly been a boon as it keeps us connected with our family and friends. But we often run into many such incidents where the irrational use of mobile phones or different applications out-turn it to be a curse. I have witnessed one such sad hap that terrifies me till date.

Mohan hailed from a family of artisans, who were now striving to meet their basic needs. Living in a small village in Odisha, he always aspired to move to a big city someday. It was the time of harvest festival and his friend Shiva, who works in Visakhapatnam, was here to celebrate the fete with his family. Both the friends met after a long time and had a heart-to-heart conversation. Amidst their talk, Shiva offered, "Mohan I work in a factory that manufactures household plastic items. There is a requirement of more staff in the factory. If you are interested, I will talk to my Sir about it". Mohan's eyes brightened up as this would make his dream come true. He was in high spirits and agreed without giving a second thought. His mother was quite apprehensive but she too gave her consent as the family was in need of money. Both the friends left for the city and soon Mohan was also an employee of the factory.

Mohan was trained to handle a semi-automatic machine that

was manufacturing the lid of a plastic box. In this procedure, the polymer granules are fed into the machine and then subjected to heat and pressure to take the desired shape of the article. The mould gets opened and the lid has to be manually taken out. The person operating this needs to be quick and alert as the mould gets closed once it has been unlocked after removing the lid. Mohan acquired the required skills and took the responsibility of this process. He was appreciated by one and all for his sincerity and commitment towards the job.

A month passed and he received his first salary. He was elated and sent half the amount to his family and with the other half he bought his first smartphone. This one deed turned his life upside down. Like numerous other youngsters, he too fell the victim of **Social Media Addiction**. He was constantly active on different messenger and social networking applications. Though against the rules, he carried his cell phone to his work. He was often reprimanded by his senior employees but he shut his eyes to their warnings.

One day he was working as usual in the production and was quickly removing the lids from the mould. All at once, he was distracted by the beep of his phone. He peeped into it, simultaneously working on the machine. Within a fraction of seconds, everything turned horrifying. His right hand got stuck into the mould. The locking mechanism was broken and his hand and wrist were crushed between the two walls of the mould. A jarring blast of lightning was sent into his brain and he squealed in pain. Shiva and others ran towards him, opened the mould and rescued his hand. The sight was full of blood and shrieks. Shiva tied a tourniquet to his hand and Mohan was rushed to the hospital. When the owner of the factory learned about it, he immediately got into action and called the best Orthopaedic and Neurosurgeon of the city. He pleaded with the doctor to save his hand at any cost. But all in vain. Despite the best efforts put by the doctor and his team, his hand could not be preserved. The nerves of his palm and forearm were so intensely damaged that his hand had to be amputated up to the elbow. The boy who was merrily living with two hands just two days ago was now left with only a left hand.

At the present time, Mohan is living in the same village, with his mother regretting every day for sending her son to the city. One wrong addiction resulted in a life-long misery. Dear readers, let us vow to protect ourselves and people around us from this dependency on different smartphone applications. Let social media be a boon and not a curse to our society.

Welcome to the world

Who can understand a mommy better than another mommy? Being a mother myself, I could truly comprehend Naina's pain when I came across her heart-wrenching story.

The wait has come to an end. The due date was no more due. Naina was rushed to the delivery room of the hospital. A few moments later, her beautiful daughter was born. The doctor called the new dad, Mohit inside, and with a twinkle in her eyes she asked, "Would you like to see your daughter?" and then placed the tiny bundle in his arms. With a rush of emotions and moist eyes, he bent over her and gently kissed her on the forehead. It was now Naina's turn to embrace the baby. Her happiness had no boundaries and she softly whispered, "*Welcome to the world,* my little princess." Naina gleefully reminisced, "Our happiness cannot be described as the part of us had literally brought to life, and we named our new life *Amaya*".

Days passed by so quickly. Each and every milestone of Amaya, though quite delayed from other children of her age, brought them immense pride and joy. But their happiness did not last long. She turned two and they celebrated her birthday in a grand affair, with family and friends. Next day, Amaya had a fever and a cold. Naina took her to the doctor and she prescribed her medicines for five days. But her fever did not reduce even after a week and so the parents visited the doctor again. She advised for some tests for Amaya to be carried out straight away. Thus, a series of tests such as 'blood peripheral smear' and 'bone marrow aspiration' were performed. Reports arrived and doctor called the parents to her cabin. With a sombre face she said, "I regret to inform you that Amaya has been diagnosed with Leukaemia". The couple instantly froze, not believing what they just heard, and fumbled with words. Doctor asked them to keep calm and urged them to hospitalise the baby as early as possible. Amaya was admitted on the same day as Naina and Mohit did not want to delay her treatment anymore and expected her return to full health soon. But God seemed to be harsh on them. As the days passed by, her health kept worsening and there were no signs of improvement. Day and night, both of them sat beside their daughter with their mind oscillating between hope and hopelessness".

On the 15th day, the doctor, with a stern expression on her face, confessed, "I do not want you to keep in false hopes anymore. Amaya's health had deteriorated and there is no more possibility of her recovery. She had only a few days left." Naina grievously recalls, "those words struck like thunder in our ears and we felt crushed and betrayed. Mustering up some strength, we both came back to Amaya and hugged her for hours with tears running down our cheeks. Mohit broke down completely. I experienced the deepest pain in my heart and my soul cried out. All the wonderful moments of two years spent with her flashed in my mind within seconds. It seemed like only yesterday that she was born and made me complete. I held Amaya so close that I could actually hear her heartbeats. My grief has no end and I kept cycling around denial, anger and depression. I cursed destiny for being so cruel and wished no mother on this earth has to ever face the same. At that moment, I decided that I can and I will save no less than one mother from experiencing the same and so I decided to donate organs of Amaya. I conveyed my decision to Mohit and he strongly supported me. After consulting the hospital authorities, necessary paperwork was made and duly signed by us. Few more days passed and our last glimmer of hope extinguished. We lost our daughter forever".

Two years later:

It was early in the morning and Naina was ready to leave for 'Ray of Light foundation', which provides psycho-social support for children with cancer. The telephone rang and it was Amaya's doctor on the other side. She requested, "I want you to meet someone, could you please come down to the hospital now?" Naina agreed and reached there in no time. She approached the doctor and they exchanged pleasantries. The doctor signalled the nurse to send someone in. After a couple of minutes, a pretty girl, around four years old, stepped softly along with her mother in the room. Naina recollects, "I received strong positive vibes from the little girl and I could not take my eyes off of her. The doctor interrupted my gaze and said, "meet her, she is Shreya, the one who received your daughter Amaya's donated heart". I was awestruck and before I could speak anything, Shreya's mother hugged me expressing tremendous emotions. She said, "your daughter Amaya is an angel for us. My daughter is alive today only because of her". We both connected with each other very soon as we had been through the same pain, wherein I had lost my daughter and she almost lost her many times. I drew close to

Shreya and embraced her warmth. The doctor handed me a stethoscope and asked me to hear the heartbeats of Shreya. With trembling hands, I placed a headset in my ears and chest-piece over Shreya's chest. And then, LUB-DUB.. LUB-DUB.. Yes, it was my Amaya's heart, beating so loud, so clear! Tears rolled down my cheeks out of ambivalent emotions. I heard my daughter's heartbeat for the first time in two years. I softly whispered, "Welcome to the world again my princess!" The feeling was ineffable and I found Amaya to be still alive in Shreya."

Doctor informed Naina that Shreya suffered from a 'faulty heart valve' and she received Amaya's heart when she was 22 months old. Now Shreya runs and plays like any other child. She added that two more lives were saved by Amaya's donated liver and kidney, as her leukaemia only affected her bone marrow, and no other organs. Naina was glad that by her one right decision, from a tragedy came the most miraculous blessings.

At the end, I plead all my readers to perceive the miracle of this priceless donation. Approximately 5 lakh people die across the nation each year due to non-availability of organs. Let us all pledge for organ donation; save lives, serve humanity.

Don't go by the looks

As a kid of the 90s, a weird image of the Villain has been subconsciously fed in my mind, thanks to our Bollywood! Most of the times in our Hindi Cinema, the villain has been portrayed as a person who is ferocious, dark skinned, adorning thick stubble or moustache with a stentorian voice. Unintentionally, this had created a lasting impression in our innocent brains for their negativity.

When I was studying in 2nd standard, it happened that I went with my neighbours to attend a Birthday party of Sangeeta Auntie's nephew, Gautam. Yes, they were not just neighbours, but more of a family. Uncle and Aunt were very fond of me and I would spend most of my free time frolicking in their house. Someday, if my mom had some work, Auntie would take care of me and feed me with mouth-watering delicacies. Their ten-year-old daughter Palak and I shared a very sweet bonding but it was quite the opposite with her elder brother Rohit. It was not that we hated each other or something, but most of the time we ended up fighting for no reason, oblivious to the fact that this will lead to a big trouble one day.

After a fun-filled cake-cutting, we children settled down in the playing room. While Uncle was looking after the guests, Auntie was aiding in the kitchen. In the playroom, I got hold of a 64-piece puzzle game, but as usual, Rohit interjected in between. A dispute was raised and he brawled, "this is my cousin's party, you better leave from here". Rohit actually did not have any intentions to throw me out of the house, he just said that in anger. But I took his words seriously and left the place fuming.

I passed the first lane confidently but then I froze, literally. I was standing at the crossroads, not knowing where to go next. I lost my way to home. I began to sweat while trying to identify the path that we had taken before to be there for the birthday celebration. Nevertheless, I remained clueless. With trembling legs, I moved ahead on some unknown road, hoping to get into the right track. But, as I was walking, I was getting even more puzzled. I paused, composed myself and decided that it is better I seek someone's help.

This is when the whole Bollywood scenario came into my mind. I started looking for a person who was fair-skinned, medium built, smooth-shaven and definitely with no big moustaches, since this was the personification of 'a Hero or a Good man' imbibed by the society. I was afraid that if I asked help from a 'Bad man', he might take advantage of the situation and would kidnap me. I was partially correct in my comprehension but my perception of a bad man was certainly wrong. However, I could not think beyond this as I was subjected to that villainous image inadvertently at a very tender age.

Thus, I began to search for my so-called, Good man. After rejecting about twenty people, I finally found the type of person I was looking for. He was the owner of a small confectionary. I went to him and tried to strike the conversation. But he seemed too busy with his customers. After waiting for a couple of minutes, I softly requested, "Uncle, can you please listen to me once? I have landed into a problem." He rolled his eyes and nodded to speak, though in a little disgust. Hesitantly, I briefed him about my crisis. However, he remained indifferent and chose not to respond. I was dumbfounded by his behaviour with tears ready to flow from my eyes. Just then, a customer who was silently listening to all this, came close to me and gently asked, "Beta just tell me the area of your home, I will take you there." I was terror-stricken as this man was exactly the way I have perceived a bad man to be. He was heavily built with long grey moustaches. His black protruding eyes amplified his sombre expression. I took a shallow breath and stammered, "U..u..uncle I live in Mm..Mayur Vihar. Please just guide me the route, I will go by myself." He chuckled at my words and said, "it is quite far, come, sit on my bicycle, I will drop you home." I was afraid but I had no other way except succumbing to his offer.

I was seated on the front frame of his bicycle and he began to ride. In my throbbing heart, I was now reciting all the names of God that I could remember and was praying ardently to get me home safely. A few minutes passed, and I was in Mayur Vihar. Yes, I was near my home. I breathed a great sigh of relief and regretted my perception. He kept his words and I was with my family once again.

This whole episode taught me a lesson for life that we should never judge people by their looks. In a true sense, I learnt the meaning of the saying, *"Don't go by the looks, they can deceive"*.

It's in the past!

This is the story of a man whom I look up to, expressed in his own words.

After a number of complications and a miscarriage, my wife Sneha was pregnant again. She broke me the news in the most beautiful way one could ever think of. It was a frosty winter morning and I was still snuggled up in my blanket. Sneha came to me, gently stroked my hair and said, "wake up dear, the sun is high up in the sky!". With half opened eyes I could see she was holding a tray containing a couple of cups. Before I could ask anything, she exclaimed, "honey, let's start our morning by having tea together!" I wondered what's up with her as we never had such morning habits. However, I did not want to disappoint her and so I cheekily agreed, "Ok dear, as you wish" and rolled out of the blanket. I then noticed that there were two neatly arranged large cups containing tea and in between those two large cups, there was a tiny cup containing milk. My eyes opened wide and I looked at her, puzzled. She blushed and lowered her eyes shyly and then took out a pregnancy test strip, hidden under the bed cover. I looked at the strip excitedly and to my sheer joy, the result showed positive! Yes, there were two pink lines on it!

Sneha drew me closer and softly whispered, "Baby, we are going to have a Baby!" I was flabbergasted and was over the moon. I was at a loss for words but my teary eyes were speaking everything. I took her face in my hands, pecked her cheeks and hugged her again and again.

But the very next minute, worry overpowered my happiness. I booked an emergency appointment of a gynaecologist to check if everything was fine. Bitter experience in the past made me anxious and apprehensive. I was not ready to lose my baby once again under any circumstances. I grew extra conscious and took extra care of her. I made sure that she ate only home cooked healthy food. I personally checked that she took all her medicines on time. I refrained all our weekend outings and except for a monthly visit to the doctor, we barely moved out. Sometimes, Sneha complained to me of keeping so many restrictions on her. But I always persuaded her by saying, "Honey, it's the matter of only a few more weeks. Our little bundle of joy will arrive soon!" She would always smile and happily agree.

Days were passing by and everything was going at a smooth pace. But one thing always troubled me. I was addicted to smoking. Not that I was a chain smoker, but apart from one smoke in the day, I always needed one after dinner. Though I smoked, maintaining a considerable distance from Sneha, I always felt guilty. It always bothered me that my wife, a mother-to-be, is doing her best, but me, a father-to-be, can't quit smoking to do the least. Each day I decided that I cannot harm my family anymore and today will be the last day. But that today never arrived.

Finally, the wait was over and the big day was around the corner. My wife was rushed to the delivery room of the hospital. I was excited and nervous at the same time. I was going to be a father in a couple of minutes. Out of anxiety, I badly wanted to have a smoke. Expecting to come back much before the delivery of the baby, I ran to the smoking zone. But as soon as I took a few puffs, my cell phone rang. It was my mom. "Where are you at this time?" she yelled. I immediately threw the butt and hurried towards the delivery room. And there it was, the twinkle of my eyes, as white as snow, as soft as a cloud, my little baby boy, relaxing in the arms of his granny. I wanted to grab him immediately. But here I was, loitering and searching for the washbasin as I had cigarette smoked hands. I felt really disappointed in myself. Anyway, after a few more minutes, I was holding my baby in my arms. A myriad of emotions flooded over me. I was the happiest person on this earth. I thanked God and my wife for giving me this precious gift.

But I think destiny had decided never to make things easy for me. The doctor informed us that our baby needs to be put on a ventilator for a period of time. She explained, "your baby is a little underweight and his lungs are weak and not completely formed. Kindly do not panic. It's only for a few hours". I was blank for a while. Only one thought struck me at that moment, "it's all just because of me." My inner conscience cursed me for being so selfish and careless. I felt it's my smoking which has harmed my baby's lungs. I really don't know how far it was true but I was extremely guilty of myself. At that moment, I decided and swore will never touch cigarettes again. I had actually quit smoking that day which changed my life forever.

By divine grace, my baby was healthy soon and both mommy and the baby were released from the hospital within a week.

Now, every day he gives me a reason to live, to be happy and to smile. And yes, about smoking, *it's in the past!*

Nothing is impossible when you really decide. Addiction is a vice of the mind. Strong willpower will conquer all your weaknesses.

Miracles come in moments

I was around six years old when I went on a chilling trip to the *'Queen of Hill Stations'*, Shimla with my parents. Not just three, we were around a dozen people that included my father's friends and distant relatives. The majestic beauty of Shimla is still captured in my eyes. Even after years, the sight of snow clad mountains, high waterfalls and lush greenery is fresh in my mind. But above all, this one incident remains absolutely unforgettable.

It was the second day of our trip and we were all wandering in the streets of the city, fondly enjoying the cool breeze and spellbinding landscapes. There was lots of fun, joy and laughter together. Although each one in the group was wonderful, my favourite was the most mischievous, Uncle Vicky. In between the walk, he spotted an ice cream parlour and challenged everyone to have an ice-cream, amidst that freezing temperature. It was exciting, thus, all of us accepted the challenge and selected our favourite flavours. I picked up a cup of vanilla ice cream overloaded with chopped candied fruits. In between the talks, my dad suggested that we visit the famous State museum, for which we need to head in the left direction from the parlour. Uncle Vicky and a few others were not convinced with the idea and suggested some other places to drop in. I chose to ignore the debate and concentrate on my ice cream, unaware of the pretty serious repercussions that followed.

After collecting our respective ice creams, all of us walked out of the parlour. But to my horror, I was walking all alone and there was no one with me. I had moved in the left direction from the parlour and probably everyone else had taken the opposite route. It all happened in a fraction of a second. I was so frightened that I was petrified for a while. Not understanding what to do, I started walking in a reverse direction, trying to hold back my tears as much as I could. Meanwhile, my parents had discovered that I was not with any of the members of the group. The fun and laughter just a few moments ago had converted into cries and worries. Dad tried to compose my mom, though he himself was completely terrified. After a little discussion, it was decided that all of them will go and search for me in different directions and will meet at a common point. Uncle Vicky headed towards the announcement room for the *'Lost and Found'*.

Here, I was now beginning to panic with my whole body trembling in fear. Just then, a family from Punjab noticed me and apprehended my situation. One of them drew himself close to me and said affectionately, "Beta, first you calm down and then tell us everything in detail". I told them about the mishappening with an onslaught of ceaseless sobs. The Punjabi Uncle pacified me and then gently asked, "do you remember your address or any contact number?" My mom had earlier made me memorize the address of our home and the landline phone number (Mobile phones were not introduced to the common man by then). So, I blabbed whatever I could remember. But that did not help as we all were here in Shimla.

Uncle further asked me if I could recall the name of our inn or any landmark nearby. I thought really hard but failed to get anything specific. At that juncture, one of the women in the family observed the ice cream, which I was still holding in my hands. It was in a half-frozen state. The quick-witted auntie whispered in Uncle's ears, "Look at that ice cream. It had not completely melted yet. This means the little girl had separated from the family a short while back, and her parents might be here anytime in search of her." So the gracious family kept me engaged in their conversation.

As it is rightly said, *"Miracles come in moments"*, that day I was blessed with the one too. All of a sudden, I heard my name from a distant wail. I turned around anxiously and found my mom running towards me. I too hastened back and clung to her arms. She shrieked in extreme delight with tears racing down her cheeks. After we, the mother-daughter duo, were in control of our emotions, we looked around to thank the Punjabi Uncle. But, by then, the family had walked away quite far from us as they did not need any acknowledgement or appreciation for their generous act. We were overwhelmed and thanked The Almighty for sending those kind souls to my rescue.

From that day onwards, my mom made sure that I always carried a detailed address card with me, either in my pocket, purse or pinned to my frock. Dear readers, request you all to follow the same practice and help children be safe and happy.

Safety Pin

Saanvi was all excited to begin her college journey after successfully clearing 10th board exams with top grades. It was the first day of her new odyssey. Being a follower of simplicity, she chose to dress up in pastel pink churidars with the minimum of accessories. She quickly glanced herself in the mirror and was all set to leave. Just then, her mother, Mrs. Mugdha, entered the room. She came close to her daughter and said, "I have a gift for you dear. Promise me, you will always keep it with you." Saanvi nodded obediently, though still confused. Mrs. Mugdha opened the tiny purse in her hand and took out a golden chain from it. The strange part was that instead of a pendant, it contained a tiny, sharp *Safety Pin.* She handed it over to her daughter and insisted, “Honey, I know you may find it quite weird at this time, but believe me, it's really an important asset that needs to be with you every time.” Saanvi smiled in agreement and hurried for college, promptly putting on the chain.

Saanvi did not have the luxury to travel by car or any personal vehicle. She was supposed to get accustomed to travel by public mode of transport. She reached the bus stop, where two of her other friends were waiting to set off together for the college. The roadways bus for their destination arrived, which was already jam packed. The girls did not have any option rather than boarding it immediately. The naive young friends were subjected to some odd and obnoxious glances from men of different age groups. They looked at each other helplessly and decided to ignore it. Gradually, this became a part of their daily routine.

A month later, in the same way, Saanvi boarded the bus with her friends for the college. But this time, something worse was waiting for her. She was standing amidst a group of passengers. All of a sudden, she was startled as she could feel a hand groping her back and trying to stroke her bottom. She was anxious and embarrassed. But then she remembered the gift given by her mother. Without wasting any more seconds, she took out the safety pin and did the trick. The man shrieked aloud in pain and was stupefied, trying to figure out how he got pinned. He felt ashamed and deboarded the bus immediately. Saanvi felt a triumphant relief and thanked Mommy in her heart for the best gift ever.

When used rightly, a little safety pin can serve as a weapon to rescue from evil people and guard a woman's modesty.

I know the pain

At times in life, some maladies leave a profound effect on our minds and heart. That might be an episode with us or our loved ones.

One of my very dear friends has experienced a pain that can break a person both emotionally and mentally. But rather than succumbing to despair, she bravely fought against her illness and chose to rise above all odds. The way she dealt with the unfortunate disease teaches us how to be optimistic and cheerful in the gloomiest times. That is why I have decided to pen down her story as it's not only inspiring but also gives us awareness about some rare disease conditions.

Shabrin, a charming and soft spoken girl, was born and raised with the silver spoon in the Land of beaches, Goa. Being the youngest child in the family, she was loved and pampered by all, her life not less than a fairy tale princess! With excellence in academics, she completed her high school and was aspiring to be a fashion designer. Per contra, there was something else planned for her. One of their acquaintances from Visakhapatnam noticed her in a family event and liked her so much that they put forth a marriage proposal immediately. Her parents were not willing initially but after meeting the expected groom-to-be, Naahid, they comprehended that he was one of the nicest persons in the world and thus they could not deny the proposal. Shabrin was totally unprepared for the wedding at that point of time. Nonetheless, her father persuaded her and very soon there was ringing of the nuptial bells in Goa. Shabrin and Naahid perfectly complemented each other and were great together.

Naahid and his parents warmly welcomed the new bride in their family. She was like a daughter to them, who got married at the tender age of nineteen. So they gave her complete time and space to get accustomed to this new journey of life. However, she mingled with everyone very soon and won everyone's hearts owing to her caring and generous nature. She was happily living her marital bliss. Three years later, when she was planning to have a baby, she was diagnosed with **PCOS (polycystic ovary syndrome)**. The reason anticipated by the doctor was quite out of the blue. Accordingly, **exposure to heavy pesticides** (during a pesticide control performed at her home) **and deficiency of Vitamin D led to an adverse effect on her ovarian cycle**. It was worrying as it meant a **decrease in fertility**. However, she kept calm and kept her faith in God. A year and a half later, her faith won and she was blessed with a baby girl, whom they named, *Aksha*.

Life was beautiful and complete for my friend now. But another challenge was knocking at her door. About two years later, she experienced a striking pain in her lower back, which slowly radiated towards her neck. The condition was diagnosed as **Ankylosing Spondylitis**. She was subjected to medications and physical therapy. Meanwhile, her husband kept looking for alternate treatments. A family friend in Surat told them about a well-known **Acupressure therapy** in their city. Without any delay, they headed to Gujarat and within no time Shabrin started the therapy sessions under doctor's guidance. The treatment worked on her and she had a great relief from spondylitis pain.

Her life was back to normal again. Since marriage, owing to various reasons, this couple could hardly go out for a vacation. So this year Naahid planned a romantic trip to Maldives for their anniversary. She was overjoyed at being told the news and thought to herself that after coming back she will speak to her husband about the second child. But once again destiny had planned something else for her.

A couple of weeks before their vacation, she experienced a small lump and pain in her right breast which increased with each passing day. When Naahid discovered it, he rushed her to the doctor. Initially, she was prescribed medication for a month but it did not help. So a **Sonomammography (Breast Ultrasound)** was performed. Report arrived and the doctor informed them with a stern face that some more tests such as **FNAC** are to be carried out as there was a lump of about 5cm/2cm in size. Shabrin instantly froze, with all sorts of negative thoughts running across her mind. All the wonderful moments spent with her family flashed in her mind and she wondered what if it turned out to be C..C...Cancer! After coming home, she hugged Naahid and cried her heart out. This time she lost her calm and was too anxious about her loving daughter. She blabbed, "Promise me you will take care of Aksha if anything happens to me. Promise me you will never leave her alone. Promise me you will be in touch with my parents. Promise me you will take care of Mom-Dad, Didi, Bhaiya and most importantly yourself". Naahid, completely understanding his wife's condition, became her strength and pleaded her not to be so pessimistic and despondent.

He assured her everything will be fine soon. In the next few weeks, some more tests were performed and it was learned that the lump was **Benign (non-cancerous)**. This brought some happiness back in the family and they breathed a sigh of relief. Doctor suggested a surgery to remove the lump with the condition that it may alter the shape/size of her breast. For a young woman of her age, this was traumatic. It was nothing less than body shaming herself. So they decided to consult some more doctors before opting for this surgery.

One of the renowned neurosurgeons of the city told them that this lump was formed due to **accumulation of abscess** (collection of pus). He assured them that he will remove it by a technique wherein the abscess material will be sucked through the needle, without going for a cut. This brought back the lost smile on Shabrin's face and the procedure was scheduled for the same day at noon. The procedure began as explained earlier by inserting the needle at the abscess area. But what went unexplained was that the procedure avoided the use of any anaesthesia. This was horrifying and when the doctor sucked the abscess through the needle, she screamed out of pain. Doctor asked her to cooperate and so she mustered all her strength. She tolerated the pain up to four needles but then it became impossible for her and thus on her request, the doctor gave her local anaesthesia. A total of about FIFTEEN syringes were used during the procedure. After a couple of hours, she was released from the hospital with the assurance that there will not be any complication again. But in contrast, on the third day she felt lump and pain again. Whole procedure was repeated TWICE in a period of a week, **without the use of local anaesthesia**. Even then, her problem did not resolve. She was totally distressed and appealed her husband, “Please don’t take me to the doctor again. *I know the pain,* and believe me it’s extremely tormenting.”

Being a doting husband, Naahid could understand her situation and feel her pain. So considering all the factors, with his family's consent, he took Shabrin to her parents’ home in Goa. Her father scheduled an appointment with a well-known surgeon over there. After consultation and necessary examination, to their shock, the doctor informed them that the lump had **increased** to the size of about 6.5cm/6cm. Without any further delay, another operation was scheduled, wherein using a surgical scissor the breast was opened by making an incision of about 7 inches deep and 1.5 inches wide. The abscess material was removed and the **wound was left open** with only a dressing over the groove that needed to be changed every day. She was sent home and now everyone expected she would be fine soon as the lump has been removed by making a deep cut. But God seemed to be really testing her strength and patience. Her pain and inflammation continued and she had to go for the same operation **thrice** in just two and a half months. At the end, the groove was almost the size of a fist. But despite all that there was no sign of recovery.

The doctor now felt quite apprehensive about her case and he consulted various specialist doctors across the world. A completely new possibility was discovered, and they said that it might be **Tuberculosis of Breast**. This was concluded by the theory of exclusion and on the basis of a report that indicated the presence of **Granulomatous mastitis**.

Granulomatous mastitis is a rare chronic inflammatory breast condition with unknown cause and there is still no generally accepted optimal treatment for it. This disease can clinically mimic malignancy, which may sometimes be misdiagnosed as carcinoma.

As there is no proven treatment for it yet, she was suggested different treatment options. One of the treatments suggested to her was to go for **Tuberculosis medication**. However, the doctor cautioned her that these medicines may or may not be effective on you plus the medicines may have severe side effects. Her father disapproved of this option as it was only a trial made on the basis of doubt.

Another treatment suggested to her was **Total Mastectomy (whole breast removal)**. When the doctor told Shabrin about this, her heart sank and she was down in the dumps. She cried, "Is this I deserve after going through the pain of multiple surgeries?" She cursed herself for postponing every little thing waiting for the right day. She wished she could go back in time and erase her misfortune. At the end, she surrendered herself to The Almighty and subjected her worries to the will of the Supreme Power. And as it is said, "God's mill grinds slowly but surely", her prayers were answered this time.

Shabrin's case was being reviewed by different doctors. An Oncosurgeon, specialist in Breast Cancer, studied her case. He explained to them that a sinus tract and two lymph nodes had developed in her breast, and a surgery is necessary to remove them. Although, instead of Total Mastectomy, a **Segmental Mastectomy** can be performed. In this procedure, the lump and lymph nodes under the arm will be removed, leaving as much normal breast tissue as possible. It is also known as **Partial Mastectomy** or **Breast-Conserving Surgery**. As she is under the age of 30, it will be performed in such a way that there will be **No scar, No alteration in breast shape and No decrease in breast size**. My friend was in tears of relief but at the same time she had little uncertainity about the procedure. So, the doctor further explained to her, "tissues behind your arms will be pushed in a way that it will cover the removed part of your breast". Naahid was still quite apprehensive but she knew that going for this major surgery would be the right decision. She drew herself close to her husband, took his hands in hers and said, "Honey, I know after so many surgical failures, you are too scared to let me go for it. But understand, this surgery will make me free of these unwanted tissues." Naahid was amazed looking at the strength and positivity in his wife's eyes. He kissed her gently on the forehead and said, "OK dear, we will go for it. But, remember one thing, I hope and pray that everything will go as explained by the doctor, but God forbid if it doesn't, never body shame or underestimate yourself. My love for you will never change." Shabrin was deeply touched by his words and the respect and love for husband grew by several folds.

It's been more than a month now that the Segmental Mastectomy has been performed. Initially, there was a difference in shape and size of her right breast. But slowly, as committed by the doctor, her bust size is getting to normal. There are no scars and grooves. However, some after effects like difficulty in lifting her right arm, fatigue, loss of appetite, etc. still persist that accordingly will decrease with the time. Her life is slowly getting back to normal. Expecting for her good health and praying she doesn't have to go through the pain of anymore surgeries. Also hoping and wishing Aksha could get a sibling soon!

Dear friends, if you or any woman around you experiences any lump or pain in the breast, kindly do not panic, but at the same time, do not even ignore it. It is important that the *Right Treatment is perceived at the Right Time*. Be aware and regularly examine your breasts either on your own or by an oncologist. Remember, Early Detection is a blessing and a key to live a healthy life!

Special Couple

It was a regular chilly day. The new year was around the corner with most of the people planning for big bash celebrations. My father, who is a simple man, runs a small eatery in the main market. As usual he was at his work with the flow of customers in and out. It was around 3.00 p.m. and the lunch was about to close when a *special couple* entered the place. It wasn't the normal husband-wife duo but the one which left a lasting impression on my father.

A woman, who was in her late 20s, entered the eatery holding the hand of a man who was visually impaired. After making him comfortable on a chair, she came up to my father and pleaded, "can you give us something to eat in this amount only", extending a note of Rs.50 towards him. My dad was quite astounded looking at them. The lady appeared to be amicable, well-educated and dignified. Pertaining to my father's curious nature, he couldn't stop himself from asking the lady her whereabouts. She answered politely, "Sir, I am Seema and was working as a travel agent with a decent salary in the neighbouring city. Due to this pandemic, the agency suffered the loss and I lost my job. We are now forced to survive on my savings until I find a new one." When my father expressed regret, she instantly said, "Don't worry Sir, I have come here for an interview and hoping to get a new job soon". He felt relieved and then questioned about the man along with her. She smiled sheepishly and answered, "he is my husband, we married three years ago." Continuing with the questionnaire, my dad further enquired, "sorry to bother you so much but is yours a love marriage?". The lady was a bit surprised by the question but respecting my father's age and understanding the reason behind his interest, she explained, "Sir, let me tell you from the beginning. When I was a kid, my parents took me to different charity homes. Amongst all, the one that deeply touched my heart was an NGO working for the empowerment of visually challenged people. As I grew up, I got more and more involved with the organisation and spent the maximum time that I could with those people. For hours I had heart to heart conversations with those kind hearted souls. It hurt me to my core when I felt their pain of being deprived of this beautiful gift of vision. Gradually, I realized they don't need pity or sympathy from people like us, rather they simply need pure love and care. It was at that time that I pledged to marry and dedicate my whole life to a person with loss of vision. And thus, this is how we got hitched!".

My father was mesmerized by her words. He asked her to take the seat and served the couple with filling meals. Once done, he offered them a small financial help. But the duo denied affably saying, "Thank you so much for your concern Sir. But we cannot accept to live on mercy of others."

The husband and wife left the place but could not leave from the thoughts of my father. The unconditional love, empathy and compassion shown by the lady were truly commendable. We all need to have a tiny Seema within us to make the world a better place to live in.

And we met again

Hi! I am Aashi, an easy-going, fun loving and enthusiastic Bengali woman. I have been married for six years now and live happily in Bengaluru with my husband, Som and a three-year-old kiddo, Palash.

It was a summer break, the most interesting part of the year, as it's time when I visit my mommy's home. On the last Sunday of that month, I reached Kolkata with my son by taking an early morning flight. As soon as I deboarded the flight, a feeling of warmth engulfed me. Kolkata, a place full of fond memories for me, a place where I have grown up, a place where I have done my schooling, my graduation, and my first job, a place where a part of my heart resides. I have a lengthy list of friends here whom I plan to meet every year, although I end up meeting none. I was at the exit where my dad was eagerly waiting for us. I greeted him gleefully and after blessing me, he took Palash in his arms, showering him with hugs and kisses. We headed home in our car. I rolled down the side windows to feel the air of my city over my face. To see the places where I have been for over hundreds of times is always a sheer pleasure to my eyes. Soon we were home, 'my paradise of love'!

Next day morning, I was enjoying my favourite *cha* moment

with my mom. We Bengalis love the tea a little more when served in small earthen cups, bhar. Palash was busy running around his Grandpa. He loved being pampered and playing with his grandparents, they were simply the favourites of each other. My blissful moment was interrupted by the ring of my cell phone. To my surprise, it was a call from my University, inviting me for the Alumni meet to be held next week. I was excited at first, but anxiety followed immediately. I was conscious for the meet due to a number of reasons. Since my marriage, I haven't been in touch with my friends. I remained ignorant about most of my classmates' whereabouts. I was also conscious because though being a bright student back then, I was not too successful in my career at present. Apart from all that, my biggest concern was, *will he also come?*

After pondering for over two days, I made up my mind to attend the event as it would give me a chance to catch up with my old friends and teachers all over again. The day of the Alumni meet arrived and I chose to wear black churidars with net sleeves, going with the Chessboard theme of the event. A bit nervous, I double checked myself in the mirror before leaving. On my way to University, a number of questions popped into my mind; Will my teachers recognize me..? Who all will be joining the event..? Will my friends mock me for putting on weight..? and so on..

After a drive of about half an hour, I was at my destination. As I walked through the University grounds, a feeling of nostalgia engulfed me. All the wonderful experiences and fun that I had created here flashed in my head. Joyfully, I entered the auditorium and was very excited to see my teachers and friends all over again. My best friend Deepika spotted me first and waved me over shouting merrily, "Hey guys look, who's here! It's our class topper Aashi!" Soon I was surrounded by my old friends. Their unvaried affection astounded me. I then met all my teachers one by one. It was so nice to see all of them after so many years. I was just settling down with my girl gang that he walked in….

It was Namet, a fair and charming guy with a medium built personality. He was in the classic Oxford button-down white shirt over blue jeans, quite similar to ones that he wore in our Freshers party, and that's when I first fell in love with him. His wide and expressive deep brown eyes had always made me melt inside. After meeting his friends and teachers, he slowly walked towards us, flashing his infectious smile. Strange, as he was coming closer, my heart started pounding like crazy! This rapid racing of my heart was not for the first time though. I had felt the same when he had hugged me for the first time years ago. His warmth was still alive and fresh within me. However, I pretended to be normal and exchanged pleasantries, avoiding direct eye contact with him.

There was a time when I and Namet were madly in love with each other. We had a beautiful relationship for over five years. After graduation, I started working in a private company in the same city, whereas he chose to pursue higher studies in a University at Mumbai. We could now meet only when he would come down to Kolkata. Though we occasionally met, our love for each other did not change. But there was something else destined for us. My parents found a match for me and a meeting was fixed between both the families. I was heart-broken and shattered. At that moment of time, I felt like running to my parents and telling them everything about Namet and me. But then I composed myself. I called up Namet and told him what my parents were up to. He was in despair, his voice cracked and caught in his throat. But to my surprise, he did not utter a word. Yet, his silence said everything. He was in the middle of his Post-Graduation, he had to take up a job and build his career. It was too early for him to take the responsibility of a husband. And so understanding the circumstances, I decided to move on. I met the boy selected by my parents and soon we got engaged. Our wedding was confirmed to be held after two months. Meanwhile, Namet came down to Kolkata and I met him for one last time to bid him my final Goodbye. And after that I had never contacted him in these six years, not even for once. We parted ways and moved on. I remained completely loyal and faithful to my husband. Namet too played his part fair and never tried to disturb my marital life. And that's why today I have a beautiful marriage with a doting husband and a loving son.

Our University Principal arrived in the auditorium and in due course the event started. Despite the surrounding hustle bustle, my mind was recollecting the memories that we had together created in this University. I couldn't resist myself from looking at him again and again from the corner of my eyes. His situation was no different either. Three hours passed and it was time for lunch break. I headed to the cafeteria with Deepika, and as expected, Namet also joined us with his friend, Rohit. I was now slowly getting comfortable and normal with Namet. In our conversations, I got to know that he had espoused last year. This provided me great relief and I was glad that he is settled as well. The initial awkwardness between us was now disappearing. We exchanged our contact numbers and shared our family photographs. When we were done with our lunch, Deepika said, "Come, let's get back to the auditorium. Event might be starting anytime soon." I pleaded, "You carry on, will join you in a while". Taking the hint, Rohit and Deepika moved on, leaving me and Namet in the cafe. For a minute, there was an awkward silence between both of us. Breaking the stillness, Namet softly smiled and said, "Aashi, I am fortunate to see you again after such a long time. You are still the same". I smiled back faintly. He continued, now looking straight into my eyes, "don't take me wrong, I wanted to ask you this from long back, do you think I have cheated on you and did not take a stand when needed?" I was perplexed at his question. Understanding my confusion, he said, "It's alright if you do not want to reply. This guilt has always been haunting me. I just want to say, I am really sorry for everything." I was tongue tied and was getting quite emotional, with little mist showing up in my eyes. However, I held back my tears and said, "Namet, it hurts that it did not work for us, but I had never blamed you for this. I knew it wasn't possible for you to marry me at that point of time. In fact, I feel equally responsible for it. I did not have enough courage to speak to my parents. Things might have been different had I waited for a few more years". "Well, destiny has its own plans", Namet sighed. For the next few moments, there was a gloomy pause between us. To lighten up the environment, I said, "Come on, let's forget all this. We both are happy in our own families now, right!" Namet cheered up and replied, "Yes, absolutely! But one request, stay in touch. Don't just vanish again!" I agreed with a smile and we both joined our friends for the rest of the event.

It's been more than a year now. A few minutes of conversation at Alumni gave answers to many unanswered questions between us. I haven't contacted him after that though I agreed to be in touch. Maybe it's alright if I occasionally call him and be just good old friends, but I prefer it otherwise. My husband and family are above all else and I can never break their trust through any of my actions. However, I am glad that for once and for all, to unburden all the guilt from our hearts, *we met again*.

An Unconventional Battle

Sometimes, irrespective of how much education we have perceived or what kind of qualification we have, there are certain learnings that only 'The Creation' can teach us. The purpose and meaning of our existence, empathy and compassion, forgiveness and reconciliation, challenging and overcoming our fears, and such many more teachings are offered only in the school, called 'Life'. This is a true story of my elder brother who had fathomed an important learning from a bizarre incident.

An only son of his mother and a doting father to three girls, Amit had always fulfilled his responsibilities with love. He lost his father at an early age, and probably that pain made him an anxious introvert. His loving wife, Priya, always pushed him to open up to her but at all the times, he shied away from sharing his worries and woes. His idea of life was to keep his family free from strives and make them live in clover. Thus, he worked scrupulously, oblivious to the fact that he was slowly losing the sheen and living a monotonous life.

Apart from this, Amit had an essential trait of being a clean freak. He was finicky about his neatly organised and spotless house. Let it be a scattered pair of shoes outside the door or a few cushions slipped off from the sofa, his eyes would never miss to notice them and within the next couple of minutes, his dexterous hands would keep everything in place again.

It was the day of the festival of colors. Living in the city of beaches, the best plan to celebrate Holi was to play colors at the seaside. On the demand of kids, he took an escape from the humdrum of his life and had a joyful fiesta. Once back home, Mommy and the kids hurried to the washroom to get themselves cleaned. Meanwhile, Amit applied a thick layer of a face pack to get rid of annoying Holi color stains. It was now his turn to take a bath. But as soon as he entered the washroom, his eyes, like any other time, in constant search of dirt, spots stubborn colors splattered on the beige tiles. Exasperated at the sight, he immediately gets into action with his face pack still on. He picks up a cleaning brush, a toilet cleaner (containing hydrochloric acid as an active ingredient) and a bleaching liquid. Pouring both the liquids in quick succession, he starts cleaning the tiles and floor. This one incognizant act of Amit proved to be one of the biggest mistakes of his life.

The two agents he used for cleaning were chemically incompatible with each other. They reacted very quickly and within a very short amount of time, the bathroom was polluted with a foul, offensive and harsh odour. When asked about this incident, he ruefully recalls, "I was exposed to that poisonous gas for barely a minute but I was choked and breathless to the point that I almost passed out. I gathered all my strength and somehow came out of the washroom. Instantly, I slumped on the sofa and almost lost my consciousness. Priya rushed to me, washed my face and tried to help me out. I was given lots of water to drink as I was coughing uncontrollably with difficulty in breathing. My mom was terrified and was constantly struggling to make me vomit. Fear and panic took over everyone. I still remember the innocent face of my wife and my twelve-year-old daughter (eldest among the three), who were constantly brushing my feet and palms to provide me some comfort and to ease the severity. Analysing the situation, my wife called my brother and auntie, who lived just a few apartments away. They were home in the next few minutes. I was hastened to our family hospital with auntie and Priya by my side. My brother speeded the car as fast as he could, screaming at people to move aside and give the way, while I was helplessly watching everything around me. I could clearly witness the desperateness in my brother's eyes to get me to the hospital as soon as possible. My mom had suffered a heart disease recently, so she couldn't accompany me and had to be at home along with the kids.

That fifteen minutes' drive from my home to the hospital felt like the longest journey ever, while I felt that probably this is the end of my life. There was a moment when I went blank and numb. I couldn't see anything. All I could see from my inner soul and my heart was my mom, my daughters, my wife and my whole family. I was trembling at the mere thought of leaving them behind with only grief and bereavement. Strangely, in that fraction of minutes, I had a visual of my whole life, right from the time when I was a child to till date. My family members, relatives, friends, colleagues, almost everyone whom I have been closely associated with, all appeared in front of me. One among them, close to my heart, resided nearby. I signalled Priya to call him and she followed. I felt unconscious and I next opened my eyes in the hospital".

Upon reaching the hospital, he was taken to an emergency ward where his oxygen levels were found very low. He was advised to be shifted to the ICU and put on a ventilator immediately. Meanwhile, he was made to breath by putting over an oxygen mask. He recollects, "that moment was the most horrible moment for me. My aunt was holding my right hand, my friend was holding the left and my wife was standing by my side, in a state of shock, staring vacuously at me. I looked at her, cried out loud & begged to save me. I yelled, "I don't want to die, I want to live some more, please do something and save me Priya". While I was being shifted to the ICU, lying on the stretcher, I saw Priya standing near the door and crying with ceaseless sobs. I was then moved to the ICU. I prayed God fervently to have mercy on me and grant me one more chance to be with my family.".

His lungs started to respond normally after 3-4 hours and thus the artificial respiration was taken off. However, he was under observation for the next 24 hours with continuous intravenous administration of steroids, antibiotics and other medication. In that subconscious state, he noticed that though Priya was acting strong in front of him, she actually broke down many times and shed silent tears. He wanted to get up and express his love for her. He wanted to say, "you are and you will always remain the strongest pillar of my life". He built faith and confidence in her that she stands like a shield to his family and will guard everyone if something happens to him. He recollected all the good times which he had spent with his loved ones. He shared, "I regretted not living my life to the fullest. I wished I would have enjoyed the little things in life, as they seemed to be very big things for me now. I understood that I shouldn't have been an introvert and made my wife a partner in the ebb and flow of my life. I longed for that unconditional love of my mom and wanted to make her smile some more. Therefore, I decided if I make it once again, I will be a merrier and easy-going person."

Next day, a number of diagnostic tests were performed to check the effect of chlorine gas on his internal organs. Miraculously, everything came out to be normal and he won an unconventional battle of life. He was soon released from the hospital and was back with his family, but this time in an all new 'avatar'! He stopped taking his life too seriously and spent more quality time filled with fun with his kiddies and family. His motto of life is now to have a simple, lovable and happy life.

Mark my words, dear friends, the true essence of life is living everyday as if it is your last. We have only one life which is too short- a journey between birth and death. After a certain period of time, it shouldn't be "I could have, might have or should have". Spend it wisely in a way where we can be happy and make our loved ones happy too. So just stop worrying about meaningless things, leave the bad and collect the good. Stay blessed!

A living definition of self-respect

Just like the number of other daughters around the world, my sojourn to my mom's place was delayed for a year on account of pandemic. After a long wait of about two and half years, finally I could pay a visit to my parents' home who lived in a small town of Haryana. It was here that I met this 73 years old, vibrant, courageous, self-reliant lady having a unique charisma adorning on her amicable face. In true sense, she is a living definition of 'Self-respect'. You will understand this as you will take a route through her heart-wrenching story.

Vrinda, an only sister of six brothers, was born and brought up in Gurgaon in a well-to-do family. She had a beautiful childhood with every day more interesting than the last. She was the sunshine of her brothers who would jump in on a single ouch of hers. After she completed her schooling, her parents started looking for a suitable match for her. Soon they found the one and a Roka was held in a traditional way. When she attained the age of 18, she was married in a grand affair that marked the beginning of her new journey.

Ramji Garg, her husband, worked in a private company with a decent salary. He was a humble, kind, convivial person who lived life on his own principles. Being an adorable husband, he always respected Vrinda's dignity and appreciated her efforts in every walk of his life. This understanding and love for each other made their marriage union a bliss. Their family grew and in about nine years, they were parents to four wonderful children, two sons and two daughters.

Time flew and all her kids were grown up now. Vrinda had more free time for herself and she spent it on enriching her hobby of sewing and knitting. As per their family culture, Ramji and Vrinda married their daughters, Minu and Shalu, as soon as they passed out from high school. After marriage, Minu settled in Odisha whereas Shalu was lucky to be in her hometown. Her sasural was just a few kilometres away from her maika.

Their elder son, Vikas completed his Electrical & Electronics Engineering with high grades and thus was recruited in a well-known Power Generation Industry. He fell in love with a Gujarati girl named Mahi over there and with the consent of everyone, soon they got hitched. Within a year, they were blessed with a baby girl, whom they fondly called, Eshu.

Their younger son, Saurav was pursuing commerce and was enjoying his college days. Everything seemed to be perfect and beautiful, until..

As usual, Vikas left for the work bidding everyone bye and lovingly pecking Eshu on her chubby cheeks. Ramji and Saurav also went to their respective destinations and women of the house began winding up the daily household chores. At around noon, they received a phone call, breaking them the worst news ever. Vikas was subjected to a severe electric shock and was admitted to a nearby hospital. Upon reaching the hospital, the family learned that due to the shock, he had suffered hemiplegia, that is, complete paralysis of half of his body. Everyone was terrified and there were worries and cries all around. Doctor pleaded with them to calm down and be optimistic. He assured the family that with the advancement in medical science, cure is possible. This provided a little glimmer of hope to the family. The treatment required a huge amount of money. However, this did not stop the parents from attempting to save the life of their child. They pulled out all their resources, including immediate sale of their own house. His younger brother, Saurav, who was leaving a carefree life till now, became responsible overnight and to save the family from financial crisis, he opened a small grocery shop in the nearby market. But despite all the efforts, Vikas' condition worsened with each passing day. And after struggling for three months, he took his final shuddering breath, leaving everyone behind in utter grief.

Vrinda and family were not yet healed from the pain of losing their elder son, that they were subjected to another catastrophe. On the way back home from the shop, Saurav met with a tragic accident. The accident was so serious that it mercilessly took away his life. Saurav never came back home.

No pain is greater in this world than losing your child. Ramji and Vrinda lost their two sons in front of their eyes. Their grief had no boundaries and it cannot be rightly put in words. They were now just two living bodies with no emotions left.

Minu and Shalu tried their best to solace their parents and give them some comfort. Vikas' wife, Mahi moved to her parents' home with her daughter. There was not a single day when Vrinda did not break down. Ramji couldn't cry as he did not want his wife and daughters to be burdened anymore. He kept his grief within and that took a toll on his health.

One day even he departed and left for eternal rest in Heaven.

Vrinda, who was living happily with a complete family just some time ago, was now left all alone in misery. For a lady, nothing can be more traumatic than this. She was totally devastated, and wished for her death every day. But as universally known, time of life and death are ordained by The Almighty, and her time for the final exit was certainly far away.

After Ramji's unfortunate demise, Vrinda's brothers pleaded with her to live along with them. But foreseeing the problems and dissensions that might arise later, she denied them politely. She chose to stay back at her home and look after the shop that her younger son had established. This would not only give her livelihood but also it would allow her to preserve folk memories. Emotionally it wasn't an easy step, but gathering all her strength, with a heavy heart, she opened her son's grocery shop again. But, the shop couldn't yield high income and it became difficult for her to meet necessary expenses. She remembered about her hobby, which she cultivated years ago. Utilising that, she turned her hobby into work and started stitching for additional income. This eased her financial problems to some extent, yet it was difficult for her to pay monthly house rent. When her daughter Shalu learned about it, she did not listen to her mom anymore and brought her mom to her home. Vrinda was not happy with this, but she had no other choice. Ramji, who lived his whole life on principles, imbibed those in his wife too. She remembered how her husband never succumbed to impossible levels of hardship. He taught her to live life with dignity and grace, and to never give up on one's self-respect. So, she said to her daughter affably, "beta, I am really thankful to you and your family for all your help and support. I am ready to live at your place but I cannot accept to live at the mercy of your family." Shalu was confused and gave her mom a perplexed look. Vrinda smiled and calmly conveyed her decisions to her loving daughter.

Now Vrinda resides at Shalu's house, but only for the purpose of having a roof over her head. Using her own bathroom set, she gets ready in the morning. She goes to the shop, prays to God and then lights a lamp in front of the pictures of her husband and two sons. She then lights the stove which she had placed in the shop and prepares tea and necessary meals for herself. Whole day she stays in the shop, selling groceries, stitching and sewing. In the evening, before leaving, she again offers prayers, eats meals for the day and goes back to her daughter's home. After spending some time with her grandchildren, she goes to sleep on her own folding bed. The thing that surprised me the most was that she does not accept to have anything at her daughter's home, not even a glass of water. She had made it clear to Shalu to never ask her to drink or eat anything at her place. And not just that, she had instructed her daughters to conduct a simple funeral after her death and had separately saved money for her own cremation.

Some may find it as her ego and attitude. But when looked at from her point of view, you will certainly understand that it is her self-respect, nothing else. She painfully expressed, "I lost my husband and two sons tragically. Everyone sympathises with me and wants to help me. But in the long run, that might not be the same. No doubt, my daughters and their love for me will always be the same, but they have their own families too. I do not want anyone to point fingers at my daughters and say that your mom is surviving on someone else's hard earned money". Adorning her charismatic smile, she continues, "And moreover, though may seem old school, it would be against Ramji's principle if I depend completely on my daughters. I have never done any such act that would hurt him, and will never do so for the rest of my life."

I was awestruck and amazed by this woman's struggle. She could merrily live at her daughter's place without taking any pains to run the shop, stitch and sew, cook for herself, and so on. But she chose otherwise. She is keeping the principles of her husband and memories of dear sons alive. Salute to her strength, self-respect and integrity.

www.ingramcontent.com/pod-product-compliance
Ingram Content Group UK Ltd.
Pitfield, Milton Keynes, MK11 3LW, UK
UKHW040029200726
13854UKWH00001B/425